No one told me I was going to disappear

a novel by **J. A. Tyler**
and **John Dermot Woods**

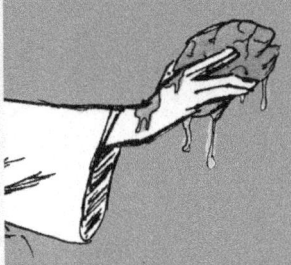

black on cream edition

No One Told Me I Was Going To Disappear

a novel by

J. A. Tyler

and

John Dermot Woods

Jaded Ibis Press
sustainable literature by digital means™
an imprint of Jaded Ibis Productions USA

ISBN: 978-1-937543-10-5

Library of Congress Control Number: 2012939081

Printed in the United States of America. No part of this book may be used or reproduced in any manner whatsoever without written permission from the publisher, except in the case of brief quotations embodied in critical articles and reviews. For information please email: questions@jadedibisproductions.com

Published by Jaded Ibis Press, *sustainable literature by digital means*™ An imprint of Jaded Ibis Productions, LLC, P.O. Box 61122, Seattle, WA USA   http://jadedibisproductions.com

Cover art and interior art by John Dermot Woods.
Cover design by Debra Di Blasi.

This book is also available in full color, digital, and fine art limited editions. Visit our website for more information.

1

2

How We Have & Make This We

We hold hand in hand because these hands in our own hands are the only hands that we have available to us. We say all of this in the name of we because the name of we is the name that we have been called. This is what we are named. We is the way it is, has been given to us, delivered.

We collide.

Inside of something there is another thing and beyond that are the things that we cannot control. This is something we cannot control. We guess on the over / under. We guess the weight of the men and women who pass us by, these men and women in passing, these people. We shut in the breath of our bodies until it is absolutely and thoroughly and for one time only the space in which we are to breathe. When the speed of certainty increases. When the language finds itself.

And the words that are our words are structured solely on the meaning of ourselves, of the we that we are, pinned entirely to us. These words that we are supposed to say because only those words would leave our mouths when we opened them to speak. As if to open them, these our mouths, would be the same as opening a door. In us the language like a closet of objects pooling at our feet, making pyramid steps for us to climb into the sky. These words, our words.

We are conjunctions.

If this were a pier, because it is, our feet would melt to the ocean below and the fish would waver around us, ripples of fish-shaped waves. If these were boardwalk stairs, because they are, we would be stepping on and our legs would pump, as they go, and the ribs that are gone from our bellies would make the room for our lungs to expand outside of us, blowing full of wind. These the same ribs that would have protected us the most were they still inside of our bodies. We, outside of our bodies, holding the hands of our hands, one in another, gripping the ceiling of this sky, holding tight to the clouds and each other.

So there is that, all of this holding.

And we try not to ask questions, us, but some questions do

come and we are obligated to ask. People passing looking at us indifferently or without eyes, hollowness, empty faces. We feel the screaming that they do not voice. Us talking to each one another's ears, our mouths moving. We stride differently. This when our two eyes watch our other two eyes and the emotions come out of us something opposite of monotonous and dry, something billowing and white. Carved.

We have moved towards all that is light. The spin of us our heads and the colors, hands in hands.

How the crowds swing past us on their own separate feet.

In our seated watching and the holding of our hands we have copied down the world in these tiny books we keep in our back pockets, us, the we that we are. The imaginary stories we pretend to create and then let escape in wisps through our teeth, salt water bowing through, spouting, if we were whales, though we aren't.

We are we, because this is what we have come to be named and called, us sitting and holding the hands that are the only hands we were ever given. The hands that we use to hold the hands of the other, a mesh of fingers that we have become a becoming.

Hold on.

We must be we because separately and apart we only amount to the marks on poles that show where the water once went, met. These places where the people drowned. All these water washed stones that people around us call sand but we know are the places of floating bodies. Because this is how we think, us our fingers and our mouths, our ears and the words we are saying and hearing, the stick-pin point of our dark eyes when they look through all this brightness.

We stay together and become we because that is what we have become. As us individually we divide and subdivide in the same image of splitting cells until the adam's apple and the breasts are the things that keep us most apart. Standing from outside of one another's smiles and having the people in-between us waving and gesturing on past the eyes that are ours.

This makes us sickly, and we whisper the wish of silence to all the un-reflected stars.

We have been watching ourselves like this, us and our eyes in the choke of this.

And the time there is, is the only time there is, and that as always is the fissure in our existence, the popcorn smell that hammers into us as our hands hold and those hands that are our hands become just the only hands that we have. Our cotton-candy faces, our jelly bean bodies, the playful chipped dreams that soak in our heads, we our mouths.

If this was love, because it is, we would burst into the blink of lights, covering our eyes with the hands that we have, un-shouldering the weights that we have been born under, these moons. Tilt-a-Whirl and Whack-a-Mole, the breathing that we have held in, the hands that hold the hands that are we.

Hand holding in our hands, come into one another like how we have and make this we.

3

4

We Have Hands That We Hold Against One Another & They Make A Shield

At first glimpse there we are dangling, our knees locked up and back over the limb of a tree and our hair, mine and yours both long, both hanging down in our faces and making a rainbow of our eyes. We grow backwards like that, at the beginning, when we started, when this was all pure and healthy, like the strangle of good waves.

Beat my head open on a rock beat my head open on a rock beat my head open on a rock.

This is what goes through our head and I say our because it is always our head and I am never waiting for you to join in. You are in me and I am in you, even when we splash differently, cut the wake in our different strides, in our heads, our one mouth un-asking all the questions. I say our when it is us and it is always us once you have come aboard. This is we though we started as two, though there was once the individual, the separation. We started out here separate. We started as two, we one. There was a me and a you when all was dark and this hadn't really started. Before we had been or become us. This now we, conjoined.

Understand there is too much to understand. I will ask questions of us, we will ask questions of we. How long has it been and how long have we been here and what is this color of eyes that we are given that looks like sky meeting cloud and the in-between? What is amidst all the things that surround us and start us and how are we expected to jump this train when it is moving so fast and the carnival of us again headed out last night and our legs had to keep running?

My hair long, tripping. Your hair a hat. My legs scales of an ocean and yours the combination of a mermaid tail. Flip the fins, dust the water with your scattering. Us and our seafaring. Us and our love. Us and our unity, the way we have come together. Love me as I love you. You love me as I love you.

We have hands that we hold against one another and they make a shield from all the things that we hear. They keep us from flapping in a wind that is composed of words, sentences. A hurricane of phrase. A caustic battering of language. They speak, they speak. Try not to listen. We always try not to listen. Stuff our ears, cotton them in. Dig a hole and jump downward, climb in, bury our heads. We can breathe one into the other's mouth and that will keep us safe. We will be the air for the other. We will use our one mouth to avoid suffocation. We will be life. That will be our continuance.

And the questions come, more questions: does this mean that we are one and we now have one heart and one liver and one brain and if I flex my fingers on my hand do the fingers on your hand move and go the same? When I am thinking that this water we stare across is a brutal stickpin of knives and the way they watch and stare is not subtle or right, is the weight that is on my shoulders then the weight on your shoulders too? Are you feeling this as I am feeling this when we sit here and open up to this world that is more two than we have ever been?

I was a boy and you were a girl and what was happening down there is the question that I would most like to ask but my mouth is your mouth and my tongue is tangled in yours and our heads they are sealed together in a bandage never removed and so I cannot ask because of this. I would regret it. We would think after the words having come out that it was regrettable. We do not want this guilt, this moment of being ill. We are not looking forward to asking these questions, if they happen to slip out of our same mouth, over our tongue, through the lips that we kiss each other with.

We begin here.

Infancy and then twilight like youth and our legs hooked up and over a branch, the limb of our existence, watching a sun regress from upside-down. Watching it push up into a ceiling made of earth, a dot of light disappearing into its scabbard.

We patty-cake and the sound is deafening. We laugh and it rocks our bodies. Our body. We are one and this only body now and there is no leaving us. Individuals we are out of breath, taken to a surface that is our unbreathable, unfocused from our outlines. This silhouette of us is a thick line that covers the entire cave wall and hurts us to look at. Yesterday you cried from it and because our eyes are these two eyes I cried too and it went on like that until we both fell asleep in each other's arms.

My heart is your heart. This heart is our heart.

We have never wanted to leave us. We have questions like what would happen to me if the me that is you was severed and it was just that half of me left there on a sidewalk in full heat baking away in loneliness? Those are the kinds of questions we have in our head but do not ask because we are wanting to keep quiet until we are just hands holding hands and everything seems like, even if it isn't, it is okay.

5

6

Laugh For Us in Our Head Because There Is Something Else Sometime Coming

Because we, we know that the sound will be bigger than either of us could have imagined, we hold our hands to our ears, not enough hands for our ears, and there is some noise then that gets through. We pray with our hands instead, folding mine on yours, yours on mine, ours on ours. My hands are your hands. I wake in the morning, we wake up, and I realize it again. I am you, you are me. At night our dreams tangle in one another, our dreams, the dreams that we have, but I still forget and you still forget, and there is always the waiting on this lip, we, the looking down into all that is bigger than us.

The sound comes and it is a rip, a tear, planes streaking by at the speed of sound, breaking open the sky. And us, standing there, grazing on the blue of our sky, we see jelly beans and candy pour out from its puncture, from the clouds that spindle down.

We are listening and we have heard, speak into our good ears, we are ready to hear finally what you have to say. Open the door. Come on inside.

Get a ticket, get a ticket. We are standing here, we are bathing. Get a ticket. Get a ticket.

In the mouth of us are the words that we want to say but when I go to say them you have already heard and when you go to respond I have already heard that too so there is no reason for us to open our mouths. Yesterday you opened your mouth and it was our mouth that popped down and a fly flew in and we swallowed it. Buzzing in our stomach that fly, that bug, bugging the insides out of us. And that is when we remembered as we sometimes forget that opening our mouth, the one mouth that we have, it is never a good thing.

We are feeding ourself with our hands, opening our mouth. Stop and stare. Watch. Glaze over.

In the future I will open one mouth and that one mouth that is my mouth only it will speak all of the things that you want to hear, and you will only hear them when I speak them because we won't be connected then, in my dreams.

We dream in color and they say sometimes that people like us, like the we that we are, dream in black and white. But we dream in rainbows and the colors that streak your face are the colors that streak mine. We cry our tears and our tears are drops of sugar-water, dyed and falling.

We live in a land of red white and blue. We live under a pledge of allegiance. We live inside of the statue of liberty. We live in a place that is as separate as we are. We are us living together.

I hear a door opening and you hear it too, because the ears that I have are the ears that you have and the words that I am thinking are somehow the words that you are thinking too. We think. We two brains made into one, or just this one brain that was never meant to be two. I think and it is the thinking of we. You think and it is the thinking of me. Us and our heads going all the time.

And bubbling underneath us is a river, and the river it swells when we think the kind of thoughts that we think to each other all of this time that we are melded. I think about being a horse and you think about being a horse. I think about the word colt and you are spelling it out. I think about the sound of horse hooves on dirt and you are smelling the dust churned by its shoes, the flowers on the side and the freedom of bobbing up and down. We are living and this is the kind of living that we do.

We pray, dear God, but the door opens and there is us again, standing looking into a mirror, the faces that face us and the things that they see. The glass they made it is thick so we don't have to listen to their words, but we see their mouths moving, we sit here, holding my hand in yours, yours in mine, holding our hands in our hands and watching as the river swells in our heads, the water, the head that is growing and that is why they guess that together we are not making the right choices. We sit and think about all the people before us, their two legs and two hands, their two arms and the gaping mouths they point at us, the arrows of words punching out, the dreams we live in.

Look down, don't look down. Look down, don't look down. Neither of us here know what to do.

I was going to ask but there is no need. Your fear is mine. We are we. There is no frightening moment that we have not experienced together. We are together. Together is the way that we have been and maybe always will be, because even when the door opens we sometimes don't understand what it is that they are saying. We hear our names, our name, and we hold our hands twirling my fingers on yours and so confused we become that they just mass, mesh, and sweat on one another as we do sometimes.

We are living, today at least, me and you, sitting here us we, the planes going once overhead, the sound of the sky ripping, and our dreams of candy rain and falling, our dreams of breaking open on a rock shore, our hopes that we will separate and yet remain together, that we will be the yolk and the white, and one of us will have to destroy this shell.

My hands are your hands and the deeds they do will have to be done simultaneously. The work that they have done already is enough, it is time for the moving on, my shoulder to your hand, your hand to mine, the us of we and the way we are thinking the same things all the time, going constantly, sitting here, dreaming of the future, our wreckage.

7

8

Because We Introduce Our Independence Our One Voice Not Free of the Other

Mouth agape our heads croon towards one another and we find in our seated posture the looking of faces toward our faces. Our face is the one face that faces out and we look and watch all the kids go by.

The kids that we watch when we are here, watching the kids go by, they are all the kids we have known when we were not kids because us, we were never kids, we went straight from something like being newborn to where we sit now, in this picture window, watching everyone else go by.

They are bright colors. We are bright with the flame on our face and our heart. A flame because we have just this one heart but two faces inside that show us what we look like. Our one mouth, because it is just our one mouth, no matter what we think or say we always just have this one face and there aren't any number of hands that we have that can do the things we want them to do. We rise up from where we sit. We rise up and go. We don't go. We would love to go but we don't. We would love to start but this is in fact where we have ended, and it is here that we sit, watching the kids go by, thinking that this pain in our neck that I feel you must feel too because we are today as always one.

There is a rush that I feel sometimes in my legs and because they are your legs I think you must feel this speeding too and then I think that because I am thinking it you must be thinking it too and so where are we except repeating everything that we have ever heard before.

A kid goes by blowing gum. A kid goes by holding cotton-candy. A kid goes by looking at our window like to see in at us but someone ushers him along. And we think that there are only two reasons for someone to usher him along. That he is either being herded by a parent who watches out for him, for this one kid, to make sure that he doesn't see what he shouldn't see, so that he doesn't see us, because we are the thing his mother knows or thinks he shouldn't see. Or that someone who keeps us here, the man with a top hat or the man with a cane or the woman who brings us sometimes water from a watering can, one of those people has told that boy, that kid, that he needs a ticket to look in this window, because what we are is something special and not just anyone can walk by and get a swallow of us.

This is what I am thinking so this is what you are thinking. What I think you think and the bright colors that are our kids are our colors. We pop and snap as we move. We, the two of us in this one ragged body that this kid, he can't see for one reason or another.

If we roamed, you and me, us, we, we would roam with our hands holding our other hands and we would breathe air that was from outside and might smell or taste like leaves on a tree. Bark like our skin rough from all the going over and a collection of all that is good. We want to steep in this, to soak. We want to flower.

Our grievances are this: we are unloved here, this brain that is yours and mine, we are unloved and it is the window in front of us that all these kids look through, that keeps us here and listing. We have tumbled to our side, we have distilled, and it is because of the glass and the looking and the schedules and the carrying of us here and left to sit and be pointed at. The running people in front of us, in front of our faces, the eyes that damage what we have left. We are deserving, us and me, you and I, we are a pair of a single unit of person, like a human being. We have wants and needs the same as all these passing by and even though a woman comes and feeds us and waters us we never, like the flowers we imagine in our one head, we never open. And this opening, when the bees would come and make of our one more and more, we are never let into it. We do not bloom, you and I, us, and we want to more than anything.

We would roam, us holding our hands and making of our mouth all the shapes of smiles that we can imagine. We would show our teeth and instead of biting like we have, the marks left on legs and bodies, we would be using them to flash a smile and show that our teeth, the teeth in our head, they are good for more than tearing at all the rules and the glass you have set before us.

The man in the hat he comes and smiles at us sometimes, but his smile wouldn't be a smile like we would give back to the world. Our smile would be a smile that would run over edges and happily dive down into the world below, because when we are here, facing our faces and seeing a faint reflection in a glass, we are thinking of running out of this castle, finding something more in our living than this ridiculous echo of us. And we are not about to make of our one mouth any more than what one mouth does.

We are fed but we are starving, and the horses that we picture in our one head are horses that we wish to be riding, horses with teeth and vibrancy, a torch that would run with us, lighting a path in darkness, and lead us into a new safe corner where we can impose on ourselves all the declarations we want, all the love we are missing, all the restlessness that we seek and find.

9

10

In the Looking Where We Look
& Our Eyes Their Meeting

If I watch you and you watch me then who is it that is watching us? We ask questions because we want answers but we are sure, the two of us, that the answers we get will not be words we want to hear.

Everyone is watching us. Everyone is looking in our direction. People pass and for us they slow until they are told they need tickets, because they all need tickets, because we aren't a free show and this is just a kind of preview. Top hat say that this is just to wet their beaks. We don't see their beaks, they are not birds, but somehow this is supposed to make sense to us.

Most of the world does not make sense to us, most of the world is disfigured. We are not disfigured, us. We are sometimes called that but we know we are beautiful, we know that we are just a different kind of beautiful. The two of us, our mouths and hands, we are cliff beautiful. We are hurricane beautiful. We are tornadic beauty. Us and our lips, our teeth, the heads we have and the mind we think with, the words we don't say because they would come out against our muscles, the looking and thinking that us we do.

Us. We have this brain that is the brain of the two of us and yet we are slow sometimes, we aren't quick sometimes, we are stuck sinking into ourselves when we should be offering answers. We don't have answers and sometimes we don't even have us a one mind to think with.

We should be running. Our legs, my legs and your legs should be moving, should be going, but we cannot. Our one brain, the thoughts that you and I we share, they are not smart thoughts or thinking, our mind is not curved into intellect like it should be and controlling our sets of legs, the too many legs that we have or the too many heads, the too much of us, it is impossible for us to grapple with. I try to think this out but can't and you are the same because you are me and we as it goes share all the weight of us.

We are lost and this is what it feels like to be us and to be lost.

Hold my heart you, this person next to me, us and we. Me and you and how we are connected. Hold my heart and I will hold yours and this will be a moment when we exist. Otherwise we are nothing. Otherwise we are something different and no longer beautiful, no longer wailing down a cliff, no longer waves and waves and waves. Otherwise we aren't happening.

I would like to shine and that means you would like to shine, because the two of us should do nothing if not shine. We should be a beacon. We should be a light. And if they do cut us open like sometimes we threaten to do, there would be light. Light would come from out of us and the world would explode. Our world would explode. We would donate our light back to this world that has given us for now only these half-seeing eyes. All the eyes we see and all the eyes we don't, because especially I can't see your eyes and you can't see mine. Because my eyes are your eyes and here we sit.

Sign a paper and we are cut in half and this ends, we end, and I no longer feel how it is that you feel when we are here in the sun. The skin on our arms warming and I would not know that this is how you feel. You could be wet with rain and I could be in snow, or we could both be in sun and one of us burning. If one of us burned then how would the other know, what would the other say, and how are these questions still coming when really it is just me talking to you and we are still we.

Still sitting, still here, the stillness in the crowds hovering, the curtains that get drawn back, because it is time to show inside, it is time to look through bars, it is time to be us, the two of us made into this we, clinging tight to one another or the whole that is.

We are slow but we know some things and the things we know are this: There is no paper to sign. It is locked in a cabinet. There is no ink in our pens and the pens they don't give us because our hands, the so many of our hands, we cannot control how they move. We try to wave and faces plunge. We try to smile and the taste in our mouth is wires. As if we have been sutured, seamed with stitches together. We were maybe at once two and were put into one, though I can't remember ever being two and if I can't recall it then you can't either because we always share these same thoughts and can't think differently, though we are a separate beauty. And the things we know, these things, they are limited and short, an uneven rain of knowing.

Us and our mind, the way we think and the eyes we use. We and our eyes and our hands groping. Our ears with their words. Our sentences and the not coming out, the unforming, the shape of our finite thinking and infinite looks, looking, us.

Just because we are asleep and with uncontrollable legs doesn't mean we aren't moved. Just because our hands, they are the hands of an infant and our mind is not sharp, that doesn't mean we need excavating, doesn't mean we are drowned out or should be, doesn't mean we should be only this kind of a tunneling, a cave, with only light at one end for us and our eyes, looking.

We are still screaming but the call it doesn't register. We are running and in our dreams, our dream, this dream we have where the world is let loose, we careen and smile and our hands wave and no one looks, because no one has anything to look at. Because we are two and being two is not being one. Being two is all of the sudden alone and endeavoring, trying and failing. We, not satisfied or satiated, thinking of being cut in two and lighted, firing out, in the dreams that we dream when all the eyes are looking, when our hearts our un-deadened, when we still are violent and visceral, beautiful.

11

12

Our Mouth Full of Running & the Wreckage We Long For in Nights

Screaming from our mouths come words that we didn't know we had. Strings of sentences that make sense only to you and me as we listen to what it is we are saying. These words. The ripping. I thought you had them in a glass box with a break in case of fire hammer hanging from it like a tool from a belt. I thought you had those hands of yours all over it. I thought it was bound up in your hair tight like a pin, keeping the bangs back, holding your thoughts in. All the words that plummet out, all the words that fall on us, out of us.

You are me and I am you and so all those things that I expected I should have looked for in my own pockets, when I was reaching for them, finding them down deep somewhere against my legs which are by every right yours.

The tempo changing, the transitions.

You are crying. I am crying. There are lakes of tears tonight and it is like when we turn our heads we can feel on our faces the texture of the sun. Like the music in our ears, in my ears and yours, it is the scraping of guitar strings. The ribbed metal of noise. Like we are back some place where there were blankets and not newspaper, barnyard acoustics, where the armrests were not fists and knuckles, elbows and knees, scrapes and blushing rouge bruises.

We dream of running, we imagine. We tank down into spiraling sad. My shoulder wet with your crying. Your ears filled with my blasphemy. We scream, you and I, me and you, us. The mouth that makes the words ours, that says it is we that do all of the screaming here, trying to reckon with it all.

We are running to catch up, dreaming to definition. Us that is this us, my mouth on yours making the sound of a kiss like the sound of a fish, and the roof that once held fingers over our bodies, our single sternum, our two necks or one, twisted together without regard.

There was a crib and a sheet, tight pulled onto a mattress. There were sea legs beneath us. Books with bright pictures and flying men, talking elephants and a circus of images. There was inside of our one head the once giggle that sent everyone rolling, that turned the heads of it all, that made of our two heads one. When we could finally grasp the spoon, feed the food to each other's mouths, this one mouth that we have, our rattle falling to a ground somewhere below us, unseen with us and our eyes.

Somehow all of it like stabbing our eyes, bound blindness. We vanished. We settled in. We fell like snow, trying to fit into this hum-drum slickness that is a wagon car careening, lumped rhythms on a track, carting us, you and me, our one body and our two bodies, back and forth across something called this great nation.

Rain falls and we hear in our head, the one head that we have, our many ears off and to the place of sides, we hear the gambling of dice that comes through walls and we hear it like it is the rain and the laughter there is the lightning and the thunder is someone winning back the money that keeps them trimming along this ride. We are kept here by paper. We are kept here by sickness. We are kept here because we, the two of us were either born together, mounted like a deer head on siding or stitched together so that when we wailed it would be the one wail that they all wanted to hear.

Wanted, us, something like being loved.

People want to hear us. No one understands what we are saying.

Tonight I think you maybe understand. Tomorrow I think you will see. Because when we sleep we probably have the same dreams. Because the dreams that I have are the beauty-less dreams that drift in and out of you. Me and you, we are like that, breathing in and out with a set of lungs that only let us expel so many words. We have so many words. We are reaching. We are a reach.

And when these clouds part we hope, you and I, to never remember back to the pacifier that was in our one mouth, the two breasts that we were two heads for, the draining drying up of a mother that we never had and could not have known. The dying stilting ill of our faces and what seems like some nights guitars smashing again wood, breaking.

I cannot hold your hand today. Your hand is miles from me. Your hand is in my mouth, trying to tear out my tongue. And my hand, it is scratching my head and then as if pretending, it curves around to strangle your neck, because if we can't be we then one of us is going to have to kill the other. If we cannot hold hands, then we will have to undo what is us. Me and you. Holding our hands is the only calm that we have, the only way that our lungful makes sense and our mouths can keep chewing down this food and going on being you and me put together and never coming apart.

Dreaming of running and never moving. Wheels beneath us, tracks. Our ears and the rain that we hear, are hearing, the die rolls and the smiling voices, the bright of a win, where someone has become something else.

We the two of us here we don't want to see those leaves on the outskirts anymore, beyond the fences, the shapes that make us think of the dress she wore and how the hands we have came unglued from hers, relieved ourselves from her burden, pinned down to this cardboard box, filed away into a world where the ice cream melts and there is always hay, the straw that surrounds us. Instead of dreaming of elephants and the stride of running we are animals in cages and the two of us, sitting here, you my mute and me your silencing, we are nothing more than attractants to the sun, the sky, which is now, as we are looking, just the thing always toppling down on us.

13

14

Like As If We & Us Could Part From Her Body Her Lips

If we could have we would have, built a fence in our mother's womb, made a wall between us that could not be severed, that was too high to climb and too dangerous to ride our horses across.

We would have bombed her uterus to keep us from being the us that would have bombed her uterus.

Us and we is something.

We are something.

The reflection that you see in the mirror is me and the reflection I see is you and I think you are thinking this too because we cannot stop anything like that.

I would say fish and you would look at me with dead eyes. My eyes dead. You deadening my eyes. We, the two of us, blindfolded and walking our legs down the lines, the cross-hairs of all of this that has become us and we.

Colored lights and fog machines, the smells like popcorn and vomit, the wagon-sized wheels turning and the sky always blue when we go, as if seasons have gone, as if this is a world that has been destroyed and rebuilt only in summer and technicolor brightness.

If we could have we would have, the two of us, made a pact that only one would survive and a duel would have ensued and either I would have shot your face off or you mine, so that only one of us would be able to use the head that is now our head and thinking thoughts that we can never keep private, so that the keys we touch on that piano are always known before we strike them, music never in surprise.

Hand grenades in our hands and holding them inside her ovaries, pressing down the levers, the pins pulled, grinning our one stupid grin at each other, the faces of our faces over the fence or the wall we have built, watching each other and counting out loud and at the same time one, two, three, ready to let go and hear right again.

We don't know what is coming now if ever, but if we could go back in time we would, to a time when we were one apart, when I was one and you were one and we could still make the choice to stick the pins in our eyes and whisper fish, fish, fish, until the blood runs out of us.

An ocean, and we would have directed its waves down her throat, our mother, so that we could have been awash in something other than us.

A thunderstorm, a head of lightning, a hurricane. If we could have we would have blasted her open and danced on her layers, our heads pulled apart and our bodies rubbing together only because we want them to and not because they are stuck that way, not because they are made into one and I have become we and you have become we and every time we stub our toe or slice our finger on a leaf of paper we both feel the same pain and only have these so many arms to hug ourselves with. Where we can just hold our own hands with our other hands and try to pretend like it is a mother cuddling us down deep in a dark warmth.

Mist spraying our faces, two sets of perfect legs dangling, the ocean open beneath us like a breast, ready to suckle and cave with us.

Me and you and here we are again awake at night because I can't sleep or because you can't sleep and any kind of separation is only pretend because we know that we is something not easily unsaid.

If we could we would make of our mother a mince meat pie and serve it to all the people who go past us here or there, boardwalks and streets, dirt paths littered with their bodies and their open mouths, ready to eat our mother down into their own bellies, to shit her up again when the time comes, and to make of this sun a mockery of the word son or daughter, of children like us who bloom into weeds or ugly faces or jagged rocks, impenetrable and sharp as cutlery.

My mouth open and yours closed or yours open and mine closed and see that is our problem, the two of us, neither one knows who the other is and finding one of us inside the two of us is something like finding a molecule of air in the sails of a ship, where the shore is more likely to come than an answer, and the pirate ships already moored there are looting the works and here we are, the two of us, unsleeping again and minds or mind wandering, making of our insides a tangle.

Our mother who art in heaven.

She either used her womb or a thread, the end burned clean with matches. She either used her cunning, born into her, or the suggestion of the man with the top hat who keeps those papers and leads us on.

Our mother was either a fish or the unspoken language of us. We strain our ears to hear, as babies, as a baby, but all we get is garbled nonsense and our hands they reach for toys that are cardboard and tape, that are carpet shards and the lint filling bellies, cavernous.

And though we don't know for sure we are certain that we can't go back, the two of us, so pushing forward is how our legs go, even without the ability to run, and all there is to dream is that our mother, she has become the sun, and that is why when it rises or sets we are always there traveling, chasing her down, this wild pack of misfits and destroyed faces, tumbling after her like something we have heard of jack and jill, where neither of us have direction except for that of gravity and a hill, where down is the only movement under these our feet.

The sun not asleep but hiding around the other side of the earth, where we can find our mother and take her head off, make of it a bowl and serve frozen grapes to the people who pass. Popcorn and cotton candy, serve them back to them those pink sausage fingers that point and those eyes that stare, looking at us like this was something we wanted and not in fact the fault of a womb we wish we could return to and war apart.

Their noise ringing in our sometimes ears, you hearing what I hear and all of it the laughter of insult and the mother smoking a cigarette, her chest drying with the two of us or our one giant mouth, sucking those bones down into the marrow.

All the reasons we want to return, the us that we have become, and use us our hands and those our fingers to peel back her eyelids and make her understand that when I say fish and you hear nothing it is because we have an impossible task, to exist together when we should be one open mouth and one closed, when we should be seeing and eyes closed, when we should be two.

This that we are, the way us is we and there is no me or you or anything beyond that wreckage of our one distorted body, shat from a womb, an exodus of fear, always the trailing of us.

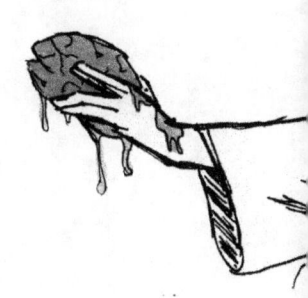

15

16

The Filling Us of a Night's Sky with These Our Exhausted Blooms

I scream at night you motherfuckers, you motherfuckers, you motherfuckers, come and when the woman she comes out of her bed, the cage and her constant resting, the woman who is all hair and spilling fur, I eat into her skin like there is nothing in the world I want more than noise to always and forever fill our ears.

A black that is my hollow eyes, your hollow eyes, our eyes, like looking into a mirror at us, our eyes looking out and into a space where we cannot breathe and so screaming, it won't come, wouldn't, the lips of us parted and never even a wind escaping. The dark that is there us in our eyes, matching the dark beneath us our lids, the bags there traveling the rails, growing down our face, long and towards our mouth that was screeching words we didn't know until we said them and then, as we do, understood completely.

Bright background logic going in our heads, the colors of this place, and the dream I was having was of living again and the dream you were having was of living again and together we were running into the sky and it was blue and flowers were blooming and the trees all leafing out. So that we could feel our toes in the water, the sun on our skin, the apples in our mouths. That taste like the world coming back to us.

I am how you feel and you are the same and isn't it, today, just like a knife.

The woman with all the hair, she shows before us or to the side sometimes even in our own little room and so people sometimes pay for tickets to both, and we try to talk with her with these words that we don't know, mumbling as we do through the one mouth that is our two mouths and coming from the jumble in our head. We say to her all the sentences as they come and mostly she just growls or faints, dogged and wolfish, because the woman with all the hair like fur down her back she passes out every day or every other from what is here called just stress, she is just fainting from stress, she just needs to keep hydrated. The man in the hat talking, his hat talking, the lid of his stovepipe opening and rusting out billows of words.

Her skin was what I wanted in my mouth, in us our mouth, when I was dreaming of the blindness lifted and the colors coming, the sky melting on my face its blue and sun, and then your hollow eyes like my hollow eyes turned to us and there we were again in space, in the blackness where there is nothing to put us our two feet on or all these hands that we have, nothing for the hundreds of our fingers to grip and roll into bars, to keep us intact, in.

Like the times when we can feel our stitches ripping, and someone has to come back and sew us up again, cover us in our special clothes, to cover our lines, because the man says who talks us down from ledges they'll think you are so pretty my dears, and that is why they stop and stare.

But no is what I am thinking and so no is what you are thinking too, because of the way my fingers are yours. They look, these people walking by or who throw money at tickets, their eyes grow to us because in our face they see all the things that they don't have to be, and it makes them smile to see that their face is not our face, and in their dreams the running of legs will carry them again at sunrise to scrambled eggs and toast, and ours only to oatmeal and only then if we agree to go, because I think and so do you that it takes us to agree to move, every step a wonder.

A thick night and when the dream pushed out and I was
screaming from my mouth, your lips curving around the
words, all you motherfuck motherfuckers and this slop heap
and you keep your own swords at your sides, you motherfuck
fuckers and then the woman with the hair was there trying
to stroke my forehead and yours with the nape of her palm,
with the outstretched envelope of fur that she rides around
in, and I grabbed her arm and bit down until beyond the
smash of hair there was blood and her screaming trumped
yours, mine, and our face was no longer the one in pain.

I clawed at my own eyes, at our eyes, when I was very little.

You clawed at our eyes when we were very little.

You clawed out my eyes when we were very little and now
these hands are all we have.

I cut our name into trees. You cut yours into my neck. I claw
out our eyes. The wounds grow.

Scars.

Tree bark and butterflies, leaves, bits of flower floating in our heads. This one head that is giant and shrinking, this one body, this one arm and one leg, all these limbs and the confusion. Some days we are an octopus. And some days we are the single branch of a tree, reaching out to a faded sun.

I claw at dreams. You sink. We are sinking.

And the woman with all that fur, with the hair of a man and then a grizzly bear, she wrapped her arm in her hand and went about crying, wailing to the world they used their one two heads and all those long fingers to beg me in, and then they took part of me away.

There is enough of her to go around.

Even the blood we taste on our lips, me blind and you feeling it on our teeth, rubbing into the bone, it is like jellybean residue, sticking to ourselves, making of us a candy.

And we think it is okay to bite the head off of things because if something had come along with teeth and razor claws we would have begged this head of ours to come off, to spill out, and all the words with it. We would have wept for a chance to be headless, strung out below a hook, ripped in half.

Trees and their baby shoots, the leaves falling, clinging to its roots.

Us dreaming of blooms and haggard eyes, hollow spaces on the inside of us, me and you and our skin.

Beg me and I will sleep with you again tonight. Beg me and we will cuddle us our two arms or all these hands together, never telling one finger apart from the other. And in the wrap of me and you maybe the dream will come back, the nature and the vibrancy, and we will go around like a carousel again, riding tigers and elephants, rumbling along, the two of us, one going up and one coming down, separated and reattached, the phantom limbs of us, the cotton candy, all these pins and needles, how we sound when the screams come out.

17

18

The You of Me & Our Film Called
Perhaps a Separation

If we made a movie of us, the two of you and me, we would be lovers because we are as close as two people can be. We are so close that we are no longer two people. We are so close that we are un-editable. We are so close that the sun, it looks at us and burns, that sun. You and me, we, I as you, the hands we have that are our hands, holding one another, listening to the hum of sleeping beasts at night.

The monsters who we talk to, the monster who we don't talk to: the woman of hair and the man six hundred feet tall. The man who weighs more than these states that we wander through and the boy whose horns grow straight out of his crooked head. All the others. All of us without names except the names they give us, the ticket stub names, the carnival names, the sticky finger names, the names we never call each other, screaming in the days when we are moved one and the other out and into rooms, our pimp the man in the black hat, the man in the top hat, the man who carts us from one window to the next, who makes the wheels below us move. The creatures we are, the two of us made one, born one, made one.

My fingers on your fingers. I can't tell my fingers from your fingers. My fingers are your fingers.

If there were a movie of us we would be lovers. My skin would dip into your skin and the canvas stretched like that would hover around us, would pool, until the two-some beast we were would become the one-some beast we are.

Yes yes yes yes yes you would yell and it would be my tongue and your teeth, my cheeks and your throat, my lungs and your figuring the words on those our lips. So we call, we are doves, yes yes yes.

Me loving you, as I love you, because we blindfold ourselves and lay in this bed together, reading through the words, I think I can, I think I can, I think I can.

We think we can, We think we can, We think we can.

There is a tug of rolling below us, our feet on waves.

Boat deck.

God, what we would do for an ocean.

Go, what we could call each other if we had names.

God, what kind of time like this we live in.

My hands reach down your throat and pull out a fist, my hand. My fingers come up with a fish, the blood at the corners of your mouth.

Your hand reaches down my throat and comes up a claw, hands clutching a page of letters, the words of god I ate when no one was looking, when you were looking, when you were watching me with our eyes or knowing what I had done because when I think it you think it and We think we can, We think we can, We think we can.

Blood from my mouth.

I wish that you would rip out our lungs. I wish that you would stretch deep and pull the bottom of us out the top, making us reverse, turning us inside out. I wish I was inside out. I wish you were inside out. We wish the two of us, the you that is me and the us that is you and I, there is a wish that we were only covered in fur and stood on a block of wood, stood on a podium, stood on a post, made to suffer only the heat through hair, the laughter through open skies. We and us wishing there was only no window, there was only no glass, no bars, no blocking us out.

Reach into me, us, pull apart all that makes us exist.

Yank my hair until the top of our head comes loose and we can scoop out all these thoughts, hollow us like a cantaloupe, a coconut, an empty bowl.

Maybe we can, Maybe we can, Maybe we can.

We run from our memories, we lace up our skin shoes on our naked feet, outrun all these dreams of flying kites and wrestling with two sets of legs and four of the most unbelievable arms. Visions of us eating with one mouth and talking with another. Swimming in an ocean where you can drift and I can stay, where I can keep still and you can drown, where the two of us we are two of us. Where the only we that we use to say we is a we that means there is something invisible connecting us, me and you.

Brother, sister.

My brother, my sister.

Us our we thinking and the hopes that we can either go or stay, the only option to shred it all up, the paper holding us together or the stitching holding us together or the mental seams holding us together or the hands holding other hands and which is mine, which is yours, the slick forgetting.

I remember.

We remember.

This is a remembering and we only want to be gone. We never want to be chained. We are fed. We don't know what it is we, you and I, us, me and you we want. I don't know what we want. You don't know what we want, but I dreamt last night that we cut ourselves so deeply that rain poured out and the world flooded and we had the chance to be some kind of new absent.

There is a remembering of birthdays, there is a remembering of looks, your look into my eyes, the eyes you have into ours.

Until we are blindfolded, until we are led blind, until I took out your eyes and put them in my head, made of your face my face, made of our face this face that we have.

Pull out my fears, dreams, thoughts. Pull out.

If you came out of me the movie would be something about violence and love, the movie would be grass and blowing wind, the movie would be a wash of red and a slickness, the movie would be.

If you pulled me out of you, there would be a movie about us two, on a screen, loving each other, making of each other a boat we can ride in, on an ocean. It would be a movie of the ocean. It would be the movie of us. If there were an us like there is not now and we could disseminate ourselves from ourselves, the us from we, the you from the I and the me, if there was, then, then, then.

19

20

Us Our Throne & These First Attempted

Yes us, this me and you, and force my eyes over your shoulder, I force my mouth into your mouth, I make my words match your words so that instead of saying two things at once we are only saying one thing at once and that is *Your move*.

Speak to us.

I cannot move and you cannot move because we two the us of we are stuck to this floor, to this cage, to these bars or this glass, to the tickets and the people and all of this our looking. I and you, you and me, the we that is looking back at so many hollowed out eyes.

If I were one and you were one you could lace your fingers together and boost me up the trunk of a tree and then I would sit on the branch above and reach out my hands to your hands and pull you up and to the limbs with me. If I were one and you were one and we were grasping holding hands that two people have instead of how it is with us and we here just the one that we are.

My eyes blue, the ocean blue, the ocean we see in passing, in going from one place to another, in the never-ending never-stopping railroad that is our bodies and this train, our one mouth and the Chug-a-chug-a-choo-choo.

And am I spinning out and are you folding over or in and is there a third of us because if the you and me that makes this our we becomes a you and a me and a her or a him or another in any shape or form I will not make it, we will not make it, we will shred and there will be nothing left but follicles and skin, a sagging devastation of us.

Hear the rain outside, ping. Hear the snow, the silence. Here the sun coming down and all the blood running out of your mouth, your eyes, my mouth and my eyes and our hands holding our words in and not divulging our plans because today in the rain the snow the sun is the day that we take shape, the day we peel away, the moment we become like being apart.

Hear the sounds of our mouths talking low and underneath

it all, this our one mouth and the things that we say and the secrets that we keep.

Hear us.

Hear *Yes*.

Here is our plan and our plan involves me taking the part that is you and dividing it from the part that is me and because we both of us know that we are indefinable and cannot make these judgments on our own instead we will just pull pull pull until we feel the pain in my chest or your chest or my leg or your leg and the move on to the finish. I will have an arm and a leg and you will have an arm and a leg and the ground will be a pincushion of staples and thread, you stitching me up and me stitching you up and then both of us propping one another up and out of our half-mouths saying two things at once like yes and no or stop and go or please and don't. Because I want different things than you want and you want different things than I want and we are so tired of closing us our hands over these those eyes and making the world dark because in our one head the thoughts rage on and there is no way to stop them.

The girl with the fur she cried *Blood* and everyone came rushing in and we the two of us haven't torn completely and we don't know how it was that this girl covered in fur was able to get past her beard those words to anyone's ears like the man in the black top hat or the man with the chains or the man with the sledgehammer and the needles because to us in these our ears she meant *Blood* but it came out *Bfflflðððth.*

Me and you and us and we on the floor then spilling entrails and maybe dying but probably not because the man in the white coat he is the doctor and the doctor knows how to keep us sewn together and that is what he does, is sew us back together, though he doesn't know and can't see that on the inside of me where you exist and where the two of us whisper we we we there is already too much of a tear to stop from ripping and as soon as this our world it settles back down we will separate and they will never see it coming, us in our panicked and brilliant eyes, mine the blue and yours the red, yours the blue and mine the red, the mixing together and then us and we and purple and bruising.

The sound of laughter in this our head, the screaming from our mouth, the blood from our heads.

Spillage.

What is this someone asks or it sounds like they do in our these ears like a question that has rattled in this these heads since the day we were born attached or melded or the day we were made to one or the time in the past if there was a time in the past right when the conjoining occurred and the voices lined up and the rhythm that we know now started.

Put me in you they always want to put you in me they always want to put us one of us on top of the other and smash down with their fists or their words until we are just the one that speaks in two shattered voices and cannot release itself. We will take us away from you and me, we will take the us that is we and we will make it split up and becoming entirely otherly and no longer any resemblance of we or us or this.

Chug-a-chug-a.

Hear this our train. Wear this our crown. We are splitting inside.

Choo-choo.

21

22

Asking Away the Night Because of Now The Feeling I & We Are Not

We, we are confused. We, we are confused and I am waiting to see what it is that is happening, which means you are waiting to see too, because what I see is what you see and if I fall down running you are tumbling after me.

Jack and Jill is a story we heard when we were kids. We are kids. When I was a boy and you were a girl, when we were the I the you that is the me and the me that is the you and the time that we were not connected if there was a time when we were not connected. If there was a time.

Connect us, these dots, we grow together.

There was a doctor with thread sewing and running his fingers smooth down our new legs the one two legs that we

95

have and the finite smooth of what is missing. Doctor in a white coat, doctor in a wrinkled face, doctor doctor. Can you take us, the once two of us, the one of us, back into two again?

Knock on the door and the now of now a new doctor this doctor here with us all the time and the hands of his hands holding us our one heart and still somehow the beating in our hearts, our heart, the us of we and you and me sitting here in this cage.

A bird flies by the window. A telephone pole goes by the window. The train rolls our window by the world.

But you are not in this cage and I am in this cage and was it last night that we came thundering apart and I just don't remember it in the half of this brain that is left?

These are all questions, our us and the we of our questions.

Are there lines still handing you money to see you stand on two legs with two arms with a neck heaviness lighted now with my head no longer taking up all the space of you and me and us together?

Am I a head in this cavern of a train, rails to new towns?

This is another question that now I have.

And if I am a head separate from your body, is your body then underneath me, your legs holding up your torso and my face topping it, screeching rough confusion from the pinnacle of your shoulders of your reaching arms of your embittered cavities?

Was there a world last night that I wasn't a part of?

Your cheeks my cheeks the crying tears I feel the crying tears you have and the smoky underneath of our eyes because there is a picture to be taken and they want to sell more tickets, they want to sell more watching eyes, they want something more for us than what has been the us of we and the taking place that we have taken place in.

I hear a ringing do you hear a ringing too?

I thought I was out of questions.

We hear ringing in our brains or is it one brain and is it my brain and are you outside of these bars that I am reaching through?

The doctor he holds in his hand a heart, he holds in his hands our heart and I we see the candle flame flickering the call of prayer and this doctor he might be the figures of Jesus we saw earlier, he might be the face of the man staggering back into us, me, the you and me that is we, the pains of contraction that we feel when they pulled us apart like taffy.

Did they pull us apart like taffy?

There is money changing hands but I don't know we don't know if the hands are your hands or my hands or is that the hands of someone else? Are those the hands of the man with the horn or the woman covered in bearded fur or the smallest man in the world and his tiny bride?

All at once we and us feeling like me is feeling like you and me is feeling like something separate and the doctor standing beside our cage my cage holding our us this heart and only looking down at what could have been.

We are hearing the roll of train wheels on train tracks, we are hearing the ringing of a bone saw in the back of our necks, we are hearing the Doctor here who is Jesus who is standing over the ticked line who is reinterpreting how we exist and him saying nothing but looking down on us.

We our this world and astounded by our brevity.

Is this the us of we that is questioning all of these things or is the us of we now the I and the you and your hand holding the outside of bars and mine holding the inside of a cage and the doctor holding our heart and finally for once and now deciding who of us it is that gets to own the way we love.

Like I was the dirty half and have been cut away.

There was supposed to be a split in two but instead I am afraid it was me being culled from you, me being corralled.

Clapping hands in my ears are they in your ears? Clapping hands in front of my eyes and are they inside the front of your eyes too? Do you see them? Because for the first time I am feeling more I than we and am having trouble knowing that what you feel is what I feel and that we are connected dots and not separated and not troubled apart and not living now as two inside of one and the clapping hands the applause the result of godly surgery taking us into one full and good and whole you and one harsh angst-ridden scattered pile of pieces me.

Jack fell down, broke his crown. Jump from the cliff. Split the us of me and you open. Shred we.

I have the us and we questions down in my chest, and you for once seem to be looking the other way.

23

24

Fingers, Colored Screams & We Us Used To Make What Kept Our Heads From This World

My god we think but we don't have a god or is my god your god or the god that we scream for just maybe now the notion of having heads on our bodies, this body of yours and mine, and where is it that we are going?

These are more questions.

We, the time of us and me, we are through with questions.

But one more:

Is this happening?

I scream and the words are gibberish. I scream but the mouth that is mine is on a head that isn't mine anymore, that is detached anymore, that is on the floor. There is a man. There is a man in a top hat. There is a man on a cross. There is a man wearing a coat. There is a train moving and there are always those and these people watching us, making eyes at us, me and you and our one set of eyes that see the one and same thing or two different things or the same thing in two different rainbow colors.

There is a truth buried in this our head, me and yours and how much of this is real is how much of this is colored.

He bows, the man in the top hat the doctor in a lab coat the Jesus statue weeping nails and bloody prayers, fingers clasped together, seamed as we us should be, me and you.

Take my shirt off and see the ripples of your chest, the way we might now the two of us be one torso or two.

Lift off my head and we lift off your head. Lift off my head and there are streetlights and maybe snow on a city. Lift off my head and maybe underneath is not summer or weeds tangled in brush but iced branches and frosted guttered homes. Lift off my head and maybe underneath it is a home that you are living in, that you are sitting in on a couch reading a newspaper by a fire burning up this me from inside and the smoke pouring out of my face.

Lift off my head top hat doctor Jesus figurine in the corner looking down at our floor like the blood there is nothing less than water spilled from a broken open emptying out fish tank.

What happened to the ocean is that we gulped and breathed and swallowed it all and the feet that we once dangled above it are now out on a table are now down on the ground are now tripped up on themselves and when I move my finger I don't know if your finger moves or even if you hear this us we thought that maybe only I am having.

There is a train and it speeds.

There is a train and it makes rattling noises over tracks.

There is a train and we have lifted off my head to search for yours underneath it.

I thought we would be split down the middle.

I scream in rainbows.

There is a man in our corner and he does nothing to help.

Help is what I might scream if my face it had any attachment left to a brain that could think and think these thoughts that are you and me and all washed together as they once were.

There are seams going down this our body, the body that you and I have, we have, inhabited from the beginning or from when we were sewn together, into the thoughts that are our thoughts when we think them, when this mouth that is yours and mine and ours it is not screaming in shattered string colors.

There is a seam.

Why didn't they use the seam?

There is a seam and instead this us and mine head is in us and our hands, on the shoulders that were our shoulders and now I think we may be just you and if so the me is where I am going and I want to know more about this kind of a path.

I don't know where the me that is me will go with the ocean gone and this head floating off of the bodies that it loved.

I did love your body.

I did love our body.

There is still a body here but it is changed and maybe now for me I am seeing you and that is something that us and we can't handle.

I can't handle this.

String up a needle, we are coming back again. String up the yarn, the thread, the lines. Make a fist and punch it through a metal rod and make that metal rod sharp on one end and sew us back together. We are separate or I feel apart and I want to feel inside again.

Us and we and the I that is you.

I am bleeding but you don't feel anything running out.

This is how I stay connected.

Have I stayed connected?

A gesture in the hands says this is done but I don't want this to be done and if I am still you and you are still me and there is still something called us or something called we then scream the rainbow scream that is colored and bright and startling and they will come running and they will reattach my thoughts to your thoughts and then when

I move my finger you will move your finger and we can go back to the people all of them their tickets in hand watching us and wondering where it was that we went wrong.

I don't feel right in this, your head below my head, my head on your head, my head as a mask on your head, my head as a helmet to your head and then as if talking to myself is actually now talking to myself and not someone else.

The train tracks are rambling words. I don't know the words. The words I am using are a scream. The words I am using are a mask. I don't want to be the mask to your mask. I want us to wear the same mask. I want us to mask the same thing, to be the same mask, to think that when we move our fingers we are moving our fingers.

This us and we that we are or are not anymore.

25

26

My Head Now is the Head You Can Imagine Being a Fort to Defend

We were us there at the beginning me and you, the us that is we, and I don't know how this we us became I. There were two of us at this beginning. There was one of us. We were one of us. We were something that was like having two but having one, was having one but being two. I held my hand out and yours held it. I held my hand out and you held yours up. I held my hand up and you reached into me and took my heart out and showed it to my face and the we that is us started to breathe.

Monster is what comes in my head and your mouth makes the shape of a melon, your mouth makes the shape of the word Doctor, you mouth makes the shape of the words that mean I am when I say you and me and us and we.

I am ramming my finger into you and do you feel me stirring your veins like I did before?

A question that I ask is a question that you can answer.

Are you going to answer?

When my head is off and hanging I will feel like this is all we could have done and us and you and me we will be at an end. That is my face hanging off a television antenna. That is my face hanging off a tree branch. That is my face hanging out of your mouth.

I feel consumed. I feel like I was eaten like I was swallowed like I was scattered and you in your hands looking like mine you picked us up and pieced us back together and drained them up and over your mouth and drank me down.

Swirl then and be inside.

Us and you and me.

Down deep I think that we are still we and when I speak the word the word is you and you bend your finger and the joints in me they creak with movement. There is a crack when you open your knuckles, there is a bloodstain where I used to sleep, my face over there in the corner.

A rainbow is only good to look at through the eyes that were the us and we eyes, and now that they are I think just mine and not seeing anything other than a scatter of colors and a receding figure in the distance they are useless.

You look like my brother. You look like my sister. You look like me I think but there is no mirror here and all I feel down my arms my chest my legs to these stitches that saddle us up, the horse that was we and is now the indelicate balance of you and me apart from each other.

Watch your step, those are my lungs you are puncturing. Careful of the liver, the heart, the tongue, these careful steps that you need to take to get over me.

The clack and rattle of train wheels on train tracks and now the reality of me and us is that I am not sure I exist.

Down deep my feet are in a new ocean, the fish only parts of you swimming my ankles, the child in me looking up at you, the child in you looking up at me, and the tricycle that our top heavy body used to ride when I was inside of you and you were inside of me and making a rainbow was as easy as dragging out only each and every crayon.

Your fish eyes my gills, your fish arms my feet walking. Think back to all the time on the dock. Think back to all the time on the tracks. Think back to all the times in my head.

I bend my leg and you are talking about love. I move my arm and you are looking away. I shrug my shoulders and I think there is no head there any more.

You and me and us and we.

There was a sense of family when I could hear your thoughts or when my thoughts were your thoughts or when I still had a face and a mouth by which to speak and arms that when flailing were both of our us arms flailing and not just that image of me wildly standing or grown still, making a shadow of one on this no more us and we horizon.

If this is how it is now and us is I and there is now a you then you are going to be the one to tell them that I have been shredded away and am faceless in the corner watching the world in windows and going by. You are going to be the one to tell the world that there is no us or we and all the fish are going to need to go away, to swim away, because I don't want to look at their two eyes anymore, their looking back at me and all the water splashing down our used to be rainbows anymore.

I wanted to be apart, and you were me and I was you so we wanted to be apart too, we wanted to be separated, but no one said that you would get the mind and I would be left with the heart, no one said that when we separated we would be separated and I wouldn't be able to think with you anymore or know that I existed. No one told me I would disappear.

If there is no we in the us or now we are just you and me then you are going to be the one who will tell those people looking on, tip-toeing up to our two industrial bodies, explaining how it is that I became a ghost.

Pick up my face, put it back on my head when you find, it is rolling nearby, it is lost but the sea will, with its tide, return it to your hands or mine or ours.

I don't know what your hands are doing but could they be searching the sands for my heart? Could they keep an eye on the water coming back at us? Could they pretend that once again we were one again and there would be something like a body reappearing?

Madness no one told me of. What didn't you tell me of madness. Why didn't you say something when us our two we heads were one head and the things you thought were the things that I thought too?

You be the one to tell how this has gone. Use that mouth that is just your mouth now to make words that I can't think of or pretend to know. Predict the future, go ahead, I will stand away here, scenes in windows, the distance all of the sudden propped on my shoulders in place of a head, a face, the world I once was when we were we and us meant something more than stitches, finite connections, your towing my head around on shoulders.

27

28

To Slowly Puddle in This Kind Of Lonely Emptied Room

I you me we were, was. This is an us that has grown legs. This is a we that cowers. This is the you I and us we and the they that was looked at. Me here in our cages, we behind glass, a top hat man and the drive of being stitched together, shut in, crammed down into the porthole of kid faces and stuck out tongue, where nothing is seen.

Get a ticket. Last chance. The breaking is on.

You have been alive longer than me. I have been dead since yesterday. This was how we took off the me of our mask.

I couldn't do anything and you as me were painless too. Until they wanted us separate, or the sky broke us apart, or the one hand pulling one half finally worked to shred us.

This was not my doing, though I can't tell if it was yours. What you are thinking is no longer rolling out to me like on a tongue.

A train hiccups rhythms and we shake words down in this our two mouths now facing one another, sharing us our one breath, my us our never thinking that we could be two mouths kissing rampantly back at one another.

I remember a deck made of wood and an ocean made of water and these all the fish that were are made of us and we these hearts, our heart, hanging up now on a sun to dry, hanging on the clouds to swing, hanging on the waters to wave and pitch and roll and flounder. Us our fish and the we that is our fish mouth and our fish eyes and the fish running through waters. I remember thinking pain and you wincing, I remember thinking remember and you and us remembering. I remember asking you questions in my us our head and the we of us answering and neither having to work on opening that one mouth that was our mouth and that we used to breathe and think through. How our words were the words of just that mouth, our mouth, and the lips that they spoke we us our thoughts.

This was when we thought: no.

This was when we thought: tear.

This was when we thought: split.

This was when we thought: There is more to this than there is.

We being shuttled place to place and all the eyes and all the fish and all the docks and all the remembering. Tilt-a-whirl blur, kaleidoscope sunsets, rises, the world pooling at our center. We used to have a center. The center now it is in your hands which are not my hands and which I can't control and that dig a hole for your heart in your chest and bury it away and where I can no longer see it beating.

This is our we, what was, when we were us and there was an our to kiss and cradle and love.

Down to this, us, no more stitching to rupture.

There was the train that screamed as it went and carried this our us body and when the lines forged apart we sank in water, your engine going west and my cars south, you to mountains and me to where it is dark and still and sad. This the room I have come to, me by myself and you outside of the door or gone or where I can't see you anymore.

I don't know where we have gone.

Gather me in your arms, I have never felt your arms not being my arms or the arms that are ours. Smother me in your talk. Liquid me in your blood. This is how we come together.

I am drained.

I remember sun hot and us melting. I remember rainbows swelled with screeching words, verbs, the actions of our two arms making of them shaped-heart. I remember jumping us off a cliff and the fish kissing our eyes.

I have no more questions left, but do you remember us?

Cradle me in your bones. Cuddle me in the wind of your lungs. Grapple my eyes into your head and bring this back to how it used to be. Bring this back to when we two were one and there was no link between except that everything was a link and there was no wreckage, we were absolute. Go back to there. Be in the past. This one of us now two.

Am I of us the only me that wants this back?

This is an us wish: Swing me and you from these stars and chug down nightly words until what we spit back out is a phrase that means we are in love with us again.

This is a we game: Scatter my pieces and your pieces and let all these kids their snow cones in hand pick us up and bring we back to our tent, to our train, in handfuls and moments.

I am still your knuckles, you are still my hands, we have still this oceaned heart even if it is only in your body now or if it is hanging as a coat on a rack in an empty house where only me and my mask and all these sutures exist.

This is the fetal version of us: Draw a straight line and it is between you and me. Draw a straight line and it is the seam by which we have been cut apart. Draw a line and I am at one end and you are at another. Draw a line and smash both me and you inside of us and turn off the lights and let us dream again of we.

We dream: a fish an ocean a cliff a rainbow.

We dream: our lips our head our hips our eyes.

We dream: these trains these tents these towns this time.

We dream: my hands holding your hands and us not knowing again for once and only which fingers are mine or yours.

We dream: us our we.

We dream: we.

29

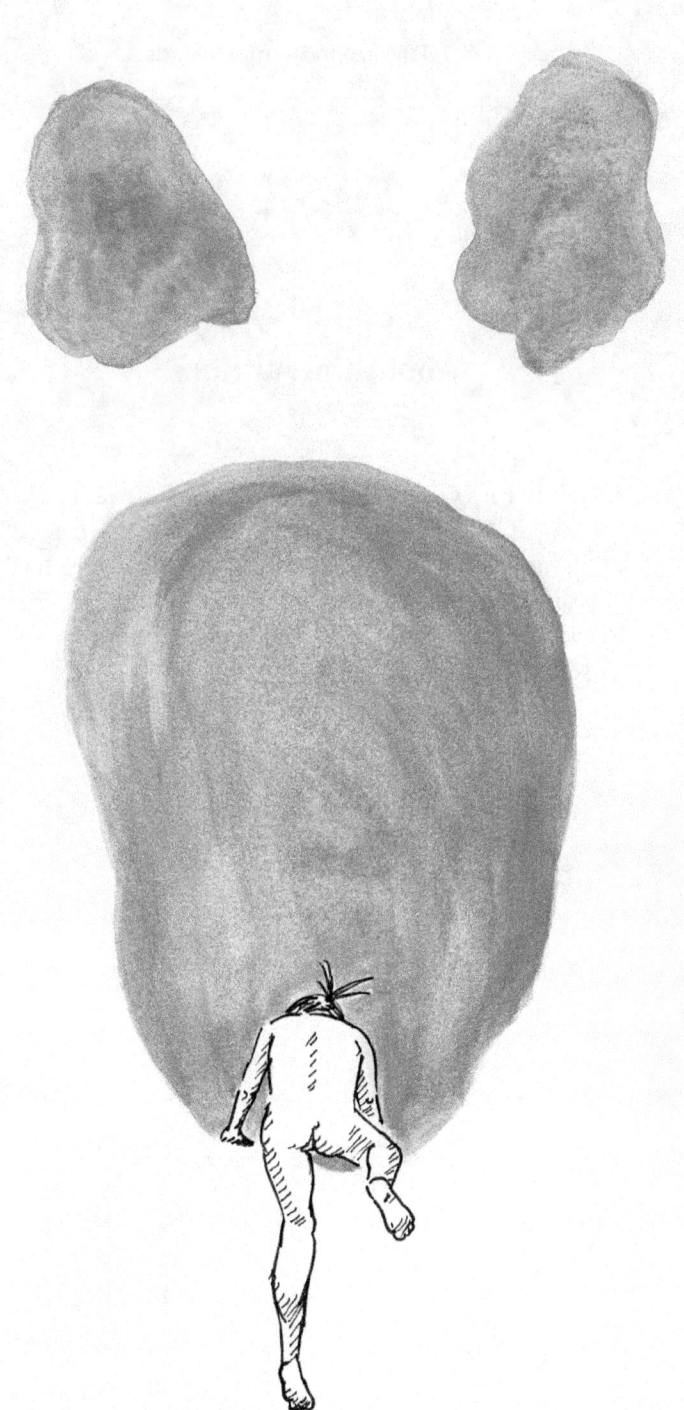

About the Author

J. A. Tyler is the author of *Inconceivable Wilson, A Man of Glass & All the Ways We Have Failed, A Shiny, Unused Heart*, and *Girl With Oars & Man Dying*. His work has appeared in *Black Warrior Review, Diagram, New York Tyrant*, and others. He is founding editor of Mud Luscious Press.

About the Author

John Dermot Woods is the author of the novel, *The Complete Collection of people, places & things*. He writes stories and draws comics in Brooklyn, New York, and edits the arts quarterly, *Action, Yes*. He also organizes the online reading series, Apostrophe Cast and is a professor in the English Department at Nassau Community College on Long Island.

This novel is available in four beautiful

editions:

✧ **full color** ✧

✧ **black and white** ✧

✧ **ebook** ✧

✧ **fine art limited edition** ✧

For more information visit our website

jadedibisproductions.com